POKÉMON

CHIKORITA AND CHUMS

BY SIMCHA WHITEHILL

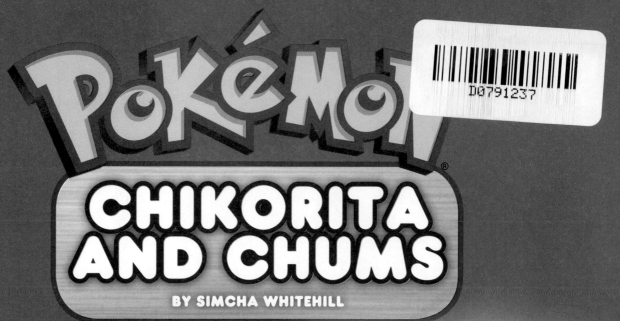

Ready to discover the world of Pokémon? Inside this book you'll meet some of the cutest, most popular Pokémon in the Johto region. Just turn the page to start your Pokémon quest.

ISBN 978-0-545-21475-9

Published by Scholastic Inc.

SCHOLASTIC and associated logos are trademarks and/or registered trademarks of Scholastic Inc.

12 11 10 9 8 7 6 5 4 3 2 1   10 11 12 13 14 15/0

Cover Design: Henry Ng   Interior Design: Kay Petronio

Printed in the U.S.A.   40
First printing. August 2010

SCHOLASTIC INC.

New York   Toronto   London   Auckland
Sydney   Mexico City   New Delhi   Hong Kong

MEET THE POKÉMON TRAINERS

Ash Ketchum is a Trainer who wants to become a Pokémon Master! His best buddy, Pikachu, is always by his side.

ASH

Brock is a breeder who knows a lot about Rock-type Pokémon. He and Ash have been pals for a long time.

BROCK

Dawn is a Coordinator who is traveling on her Pokémon journey. She has become a good friend to Ash and Brock.

DAWN

Jessie, **James**, and **Meowth** are Pokémon thieves! They steal Pokémon from other Trainers. Luckily, they aren't very good at it.

TEAM ROCKET

2

CHIKORITA
LEAF POKÉMON

STATS

Chikorita never needs to check the weather. The leaf on its head lets it know how hot and damp it is.

How to say it:
CHICK-oh-REE-ta

Type: Grass

Height: 2' 11"

Weight: 14.1 lbs.

FUN FACT — Trainers starting out in Johto can choose cheerful Chikorita as their first Pokémon.

3

CHINCHOU

ANGLER POKÉMON

4

FUN FACT

The truth about Chinchou may shock you! This harmless looking Pokémon uses its electric-charged antenna to zap foes.

CYNDAQUIL
FIRE MOUSE POKÉMON

STATS

Cyndaquil is usually shy, but when it gets scared, its back blasts ferocious flames.

How to say it:
SIN-da-kwill

Type: Fire

Height: 1' 08"

Weight: 17.4 lbs.

FUN FACT

Dawn won a Pokémon Egg in a match. It hatched into a Cyndaquil.

DUNSPARCE

LAND SNAKE POKÉMON

Dunsparce digs its own digs! Using its tail, it burrows a nest into the dirt.

How to say it:
DUN-sparce

Type: Normal

Height: 4' 11"

Weight: 30.9 lbs.

FUN FACT — **Dunsparce's wings are too tiny to help it fly, but they keep it hovering above the ground.**

GIRAFARIG
LONG NECK POKÉMON

Girafarig has eyes in the back of its head — well, actually, in its tail. Its second, smaller head looks out for trouble.

How to say it:
jir-RAFF-uh-rig

Type: Normal-Psychic

Height: 4' 11"

Weight: 91.5 lbs.

FUN FACT Beware — if Girafarig's small head smells something good, it may try to take a big bite, even if what it smells isn't food.

HOOTHOOT

OWL POKÉMON

Hoothoot cries out at the same time every day. You can set your watch by it.

How to say it:
HOOT-HOOT

Type: Normal-Flying

Height: 2' 04"

Weight: 46.7 lbs.

8

FUN FACT Hoothoot always stands on one foot—even when it's under attack.

HOPPIP
COTTONWEED POKÉMON

STATS

Hoppip drifts around from place to place, surfing on the wind.

How to say it:
HOP-pip

Type: Grass-Flying

Height: 1' 04"

Weight: 1.1 lbs.

FUN FACT Hoppip uses its tiny feet to grip the ground, but when a strong wind blows . . . up, up, and away it goes!

LEDYBA

FIVE STAR POKÉMON

STATS

Ledyba don't like being cold or alone. When winter comes, they gather in groups for warmth.

How to say it:
LEH-dee-bah

Type: Bug-Flying

Height: 3' 03"

Weight: 23.8 lbs.

FUN FACT Ledyba shows its feelings through its scent. It's so shy, it won't move unless it's with other Ledyba.

MAREEP
WOOL POKÉMON

STATS

Mareep's fluffy fleece is full of static electricity. Its wool can double in size when it's super-charged up.

How to say it:
mah-REEP

Type: Electric

Height: 2' 00"

Weight: 17.2 lbs.

In the summer, Mareep sheds its puffy coat. But within a week, it grows a full coat again.

MILTANK
MILK COW POKÉMON

Miltank's yummy milk helps kids grow up strong and healthy.

How to say it:
MIL-tank

Type: Normal

Height: 3' 11"

Weight: 166.4 lbs.

12 **FUN FACT** Feeling sick? Miltank's nutritious and delicious milk is the best medicine!

MISDREAVUS
SCREECH POKÉMON

STATS

Late at night, Misdreavus can be heard shrieking.

How to say it:
miss-DREE-vus

Type: Ghost

Height: 2' 04"

Weight: 2.2 lbs.

 **FUN FACT**

Misdreavus like to pull people's hair, then watch them jump up in fear!

NATU

TINY BIRD POKÉMON

Natu can peck food off cactus trees so gracefully, it doesn't get pricked.

How to say it:
NAH-too

Type: Psychic-Flying

Height: 0' 08"

Weight: 4.4 lbs.

14

Ash once visited a carnival tent that shrank him down to a tiny size. A Natu helped return him to normal!

QWILFISH
BALLOON POKÉMON

STATS

Qwilfish is covered in spikes that shoot poison. But it can only sting after drinking water, which puffs up its body.

How to say it:
KWIL-fish

Type: Water-Poison

Height: 1' 08"

Weight: 8.6 lbs.

FUN FACT Qwilfish's poisonous prickers evolved from scales.

15

SENTRET

SCOUT POKÉMON

STATS

Sentret uses its striped tail to stand up tall and get a good look around.

How to say it: *SEN-tret*

Type: *Normal*

Height: *2' 07"*

Weight: *13.2 lbs.*

FUN FACT Sentret can spot trouble coming from far away. It uses its shrill cry to warn its Sentret pals.

SHUCKLE
MOLD POKÉMON

STATS

To avoid enemies, Shuckle hides under rocks and stays perfectly still.

How to say it:
SHUCK-kull

Type: Bug-Rock

Height: 2' 00"

Weight: 45.2 lbs.

FUN FACT

Shuckle's red shell is its own personal smoothie machine! It stores berries and turns them into delicious fruit juice.

17

SNEASEL
SHARP CLAW POKÉMON

STATS

Sneasel only reveals its long, sharp claws when it is about to attack.

How to say it:
SNEE-zul

Type: Dark-Ice

Height: 2' 11"

Weight: 61.7 lbs.

FUN FACT

Sneaky Sneasel likes to steal eggs from nests to make its breakfast.

SPINARAK
STRING SPIT POKÉMON

Spinarak are master weavers. They can spin a strong web out of very thin thread.

How to say it:
SPIN-uh-rack

Type: Bug-Poison

Height: 1' 08"

Weight: 18.7 lbs.

 Patient Spinarak will sit still for days, waiting for prey to get stuck in their webs.

STANTLER

BIG HORN POKÉMON

Stantler's antlers seem to change reality. It makes everyone who sees it feel transported to a different place.

How to say it:
STAN-tler

Type: Normal

Height: 4' 07"

Weight: 157.0 lbs.

20

FUN FACT Whatever you do, don't stare at Stantler. Its horns will hypnotize you!

SUNKERN
SEED POKÉMON

STATS

Sunkern get all the nutrition they need from drinking dewdrops off the bottoms of leaves.

How to say it:
SUN-kern

Type: Grass

Height: 1' 00"

Weight: 4.0 lbs.

FUN FACT Sunkern sometimes fall from the sky, catching Trainers by surprise.

21

TOGEPI

SPIKE BALL POKÉMON

STATS

Happy Togepi is the color of sunshine. Its shell is stuffed with joy.

How to say it:
TOƐ-geh-pee

Type: Normal

Height: 1' 00"

Weight: 3.3 lbs.

FUN FACT Rumor has it that happiness will come to anyone who can get a sleeping Togepi to wake up.

TOTODILE
BIG JAW POKÉMON

STATS

Toothy Totodile loves to sink its chompers into anything it can — even its Trainer.

How to say it:
TOE-toe-dyle

Type: Water

Height: 2' 00"

Weight: 20.9 lbs.

 **FUN FACT** Brock once met a picky Totodile who didn't like to eat. Its food was too sweet!

TYROGUE
SCUFFLE POKÉMON

STATS

Tyrogue has a lot of energy and a very short temper. It will hit any foe without warning.

How to say it:
tie-ROAG

Type: Fighting

Height: 2' 04"

Weight: 46.3 lbs.

FUN FACT Even if it's losing, Tyrogue will keep on fighting. This helps make it stronger.